Ben Has Something to Say

A STORY ABOUT STUTTERING

WRITTEN BY **Laurie Lears**

ILLUSTRATED BY **Karen Ritz**

Albert Whitman & Company
Morton Grove, Illinois

For Parents and Teachers of Children Who Stutter
by Nina Reardon, MS, CCC-SLP

All children who stutter are different. They differ in the ways in which they stutter as well as in their feelings and attitudes regarding their speech.

Some children, like Ben, may be reluctant to speak. It is important that the adults in their lives encourage the expression of their ideas. By listening to the *message* and not the way in which it is delivered, adults can help children see that their ideas are more important than their stuttering.

As Ben discovers that what he has to say is more important than how he says it, he learns that he can communicate well whether or not he stutters. This gives him the confidence to say what he wants to say, and to gain a new friend in the process!

What Stuttering Is and Is Not:

Stuttering is a communication disorder that has long defied definitions that could encompass its complex nature. Therefore, it is important to understand what stuttering IS NOT.

Stuttering IS NOT predictable.

Stuttering IS NOT caused by parents or significant others.

Stuttering IS NOT the result of a brain defect.

Stuttering IS NOT caused by talking too fast.

Stuttering IS NOT an emotional disorder.

Stuttering IS NOT the whole of the person who stutters.

As we dispel these myths about stuttering, we realize that it is important to increase our knowledge and understanding of this disorder. Knowing the facts can help us deal more effectively with stuttering when it is a part of our families and our classrooms.

If You Know Someone Who Stutters:

Because many of you who are reading this book may know someone who stutters, the following information may be helpful to you when speaking with him or her:

* Show interest in what the person is saying, not the way in which he or she says it.

* Maintain eye contact and keep a relaxed communication style.

* Wait patiently for the person to finish. Avoid finishing his or her sentences.

* Avoid giving advice: "Slow down," "Take a deep breath," "Think about what you are going to say," etc. Such ideas are simplistic answers to a complex problem, and are not helpful to the person who stutters.

Additional resource information on stuttering can be found at the end of this book.

Ben was a good reader, but he did not like to read
aloud at school. At reading time he pretended to have a cough
and had to go to the water fountain for a drink.

During the Morning Meeting he shook his head when it was
his turn to share something special with the class.

Even at lunch he kept his nose buried in a book so he wouldn't
have to speak to the other children.

Ben did not like to talk because he stuttered.

Ben could hardly wait for Friday afternoon to arrive. That's when Dad picked him up from school and they drove to Wayne's Junkyard.

The bouncy pickup truck seemed to jiggle his words loose, and he told Dad all about his day. Dad never laughed or teased when his voice stuck and stuttered.

At the junkyard, cars, trucks, and buses were scattered about as if they'd been blown there by a strong wind. Dad scurried among the vehicles looking for parts he could use in his job as a mechanic.

"Look here!" cried Dad as he peered into a car engine. "This transmission looks like new!"

But Ben wasn't looking. Something in the corner of the junkyard had caught his eye.

He moved closer and saw a big black dog chained to a doghouse. The dog's pointed ears seemed too big for his head, and his tail swished so fast it stirred up a cloud of dust.

Mr. Wayne came out of his house and called to Ben. "You can pet Spike. He won't hurt you!"

Ben sat down on an old tire, and Spike scooted to him on his belly. He wiggled all over and licked Ben's hand.

"Y-Y-You are friendly!" said Ben. Spike put his head on Ben's lap, and Ben spoke to him softly until Dad had finished collecting the parts he needed.

"Your dog is nice," said Dad when they stopped by the office to pay Mr. Wayne.

"I'm worried he's *too* nice for a guard dog," Mr. Wayne said. "How do *you* like him?" he asked Ben.

Ben smiled, but he did not answer.

"Say, I don't believe I've ever heard you talk," said Mr. Wayne. "What's the matter, cat got your tongue?"

Ben shrugged and hurried out the door before Mr. Wayne could ask more questions.

The next week Ben brought along a rubber bone for Spike.

"You'd better check with Mr. Wayne before you give it to him," said Dad.

Ben frowned. Mr. Wayne might think there was something wrong with him if he heard the way he stuttered. He carried the bone into Mr. Wayne's office and placed it on the counter.

Mr. Wayne looked up. "What can I do for you?" he asked. Ben pointed to the bone and then out the window towards Spike. "Do you want to give that bone to my dog?" asked Mr. Wayne.

Ben nodded.

"Go ahead," said Mr. Wayne. "By golly, you *are* shy!"

Ben dashed outside to Spike. Spike danced around his feet and even tried to climb on his lap. Ben hugged him. "I'm not really shy," he said. Spike tilted his head and seemed to be listening.

When it was time for Ben to leave, Spike tried to follow. His heavy chain pulled him back, and he whimpered.

"It looks like Spike is getting attached to you," said Dad.

"He's cold and l-l-lonely," said Ben. "Next week I'll b-b-bring him a b-blanket."

On Friday Ben tucked a soft blanket under his arm.
"D-D-Dad, will you ask Mr. Wayne if I can put the b-blanket
in Sss...Spike's house?" he asked.

Dad shook his head. "You know you can't let your stuttering
keep you from talking," he said.

Of course Ben knew that! Mrs. Hanson, his speech therapist,
told him all the time. Ben stomped his foot.

"I d-don't care!" he cried. "I...I'm not t-talking until my
sss...stuttering goes away!"

"Sorry," said Dad. "But I can't talk for you."

Ben took a pencil from his book bag and wrote a note to Mr. Wayne: *Could Spike please have this blanket?*

"What do you have there?" asked Mr. Wayne.

Ben's cheeks burned as he handed him the note.

Mr. Wayne read the note. "You can give Spike the blanket," he said. "But you're spoiling that dog!"

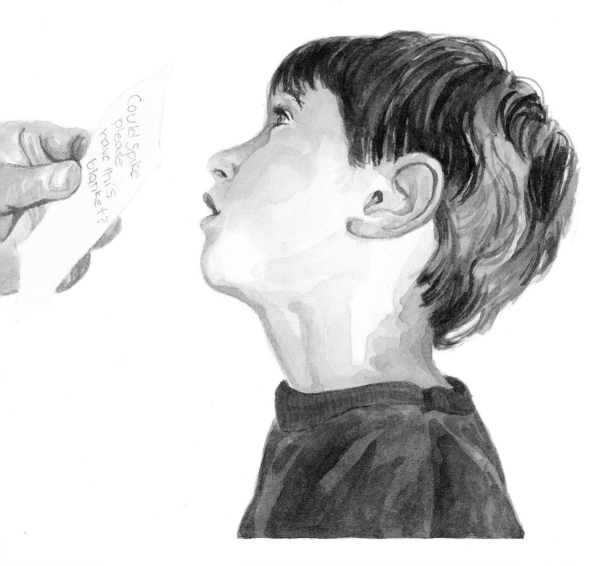

The next time Ben came to visit, Spike's water was almost
frozen. He pounded the ice loose and refilled the dish with
fresh water.

Spike trembled and pressed against Ben's legs. His fur was
dull and matted. "I…I will bring a b-b-brush for you soon,"
Ben promised. But he knew that all the brushes, blankets, and
bones in the world would not make up for the love Spike
needed.

"Sss...Spike's not h-h-happy," he told Dad on the way home.

Dad nodded. "I think Spike would rather be a pet than a guard dog," he said.

One Friday afternoon Ben could tell something was different at the junkyard. Spike cowered next to his doghouse, and Mr. Wayne paced back and forth in his office.

"I was robbed last night," said Mr. Wayne. "And that good-for-nothing dog never barked. I'm taking him to the pound and getting an alarm instead!"

Ben gasped and looked at Dad. But Dad wasn't saying anything! Ben knew it was up to him.

He took a big, shaky breath. "Sss…Spike's a g-good d-d-dog!" he cried. "I…I will b-buy him with the money I've s-s-saved!" Ben's words came out broken and jumbled, but he didn't care.

Mr. Wayne's eyes opened wide. "It's up to your dad," he said. Dad smiled and took out his wallet.

On the ride home, Spike sat between Dad and Ben. "Well," said Dad, "it seems like you changed your mind about talking."

Ben nodded. "I s-still don't like the way my voice sss...sounds when I talk. B-b-but there are sss...some things I really want to s-s-say."

"It sure paid off this time," said Dad, patting Spike's head.

Ben grinned, and decided he just might be brave enough to tell everyone at school about his new dog, Spike.

Resources

The following organizations offer free or inexpensive books,
pamphlets, videotapes, and educational programs:

Stuttering Foundation of America

3100 Walnut Grove Road, Suite 603

Memphis, TN 38111

1-800-992-9392

Email: stutter@vantek.net

Web Site: www.stuttersfa.org

National Stuttering Association

5100 East LaPalma, Suite 208

Anaheim Hills, CA 92807

1-800-364-1677

Email: nsastutter@aol.com

Web Site: www.nsastutter.org

For additional information and links to other organizations
and resources on the Internet:

The Stuttering Home Page

Minnesota State University, Mankato, MN

Web Site: www.stutteringhomepage.com

To my daughters, Heather and Beth.
And with thanks to Linda Bergdoll,
James McClure, and Wendy McClure. — L. L.

For Louie and his family. — K. R.

*

Library of Congress Cataloging-in-Publication Data
Lears, Laurie.
Ben has something to say: a story about stuttering
by Laurie Lears ; illustrated by Karen Ritz.
p. cm.
Summary: In order to help a neglected dog that he sees at a junkyard,
Ben, who stutters, begins to confront his fear of speaking.
ISBN 0-8075-0633-8
[1. Stuttering—Fiction. 2. Dogs—Fiction.] I. Ritz, Karen, ill. II.Title.
PZ7.L46365 Be 2000
[E]—dc21
99-050866

The illustrations were done in watercolor on fabreano paper.
The typeface is Bodoni Classic Hand Drawn – Medium.
The design is by Scott Piehl.